CONFIDENCE IN ACTION

A Step-by-Step Guide to Leveling UP

Marion Forbes-Segree

CONFIDENCE IN ACTION

A Step-by-Step Guide to Leveling UP

Marion Forbes-Segree

DEDICATION

"To those who have ever felt uncertain, stuck, or weighed down by doubt—this workbook is for you. Within these pages, may you rediscover your gifts, reclaim your confidence, and renew the powerful sense of self that has always been within you."

MARION FORBES
CONSULTING

Designed by Katrina M. Pablico

Introduction

Welcome to **Confidence in Action!**
This workbook is your companion as you embark on a journey to build self-confidence, overcome challenges, and embrace your full potential.

Each module offers actionable exercises, reflective tasks, and questions to help you engage deeply with your personal growth.

Modules

Module 1
Self-Awareness: Rediscovering YOU!

Exercise 1: Self-Awareness Journal

Write three adjectives that describe how you currently see yourself and three adjectives for how you want to be seen. Compare the lists

How you CURRENTLY SEE yourself

How you WANT to be SEEN

Reflection Questions

What patterns or gaps do you notice?

What actions can you take to bridge the gap?

Exercise 2: Imperfection Acceptance

List three areas in your life where you feel the need to be perfect.
For each, write one small step to embrace imperfection.

Action Step

Commit to taking one of these steps this week.

Daily Check-In Chart

Track your feelings, thoughts, and actions for one week. Use the following prompts:

Morning:

What's your FOCUS for the day?

____

____

____

____

____

____

Evening

What went well? What could be improved?

____

____

____

____

____

Module 2
Dream Big: Vision & Action

Exercise 1: Dream Visualization

Spend 10 minutes visualizing your dream life. Write down what you see, feel, and hear.

Reflection Question

What excites you most about this vision?

Task: Create a Vision Board

Gather images, quotes, and symbols that represent your dream.
Arrange them into a vision board you can refer to daily.

MY VISION BOARD

paste image here

paste image here

paste image here

paste image here

paste image here

paste image here

Exercise 2: Overcoming Doubts

Write down three doubts about your dream. For each doubt, write an empowering belief to counter it.

Three DOUBTS about your dream

EMPOWERING BELIEFS to counter it

Reflection Question

How can you strengthen these beliefs over time?

Module 3
Leap of Faith:
Conquer & Trust

Exercise 1: Fear Inventory

Write about your biggest fear related to taking a leap of faith.

Answer these questions:

- What's the worst that could happen?
- How would you handle it?

....

....

....

....

....

Task: Faith in Action

Commit to one bold action this week that aligns with your vision.

....

....

....

....

Reflection Question

How did this action make you feel, and what did you learn from it?

Module 4
From Pain to Purpose: Navigating Loss

Exercise 1: Gratitude in Pain

- Reflect on a challenging time in your life. Write about one lesson you've learned from it.

Reflection Question

How has this lesson shaped who you are today?

Task: Support Circle Map

Identify people in your life who provide emotional support. Choose one person to connect with this week.

Write their names here:

____

____

____

____

____

____

Write their names here:

____

____

____

____

____

____

Exercise 1: Opportunity Identification

Brainstorm five skills or passions. For each, list one way it could turn into a business idea.

Your Skill and Passion

Way to turn it to a Business Idea

Reflection Questions

Which idea excites you the most?

....
....
....
....
....
....
....
....
....

Task: Plan Your First Step

Outline three actionable steps to explore your chosen idea.

Legacy of Faith: Empowering Generations

Exercise 1: Legacy Letter

Write a letter to your child or grandchildren about the values you hope to pass on.

____

____

____

____

____

____

____

____

____

____

____

Reflection Questions

What legacy do you want to leave behind?

Task: Legacy Project

Choose one action this month to build your legacy (e.g., teaching a skill, starting a family tradition).

Module 7
Breaking Barriers: Overcoming Bias

Exercise 1: Bias Reflection

Write about a time you faced bias and how you overcame it.

Reflection Question

What strengths helped you navigate this challenge?

Task: Breaking Barriers

Identify one area where you feel limited by bias. Take one step to challenge this limitation.

Module 8

Purpose-Driven Vision: Clarity & Commitment

Exercise 1: Purpose Mapping

List your top five values. Reflect on how these values align with your vision.

MY Top 5 Values

1. _______________________________________

2. _______________________________________

3. _______________________________________

4. _______________________________________

5. _______________________________________

Reflection Question

What adjustments, if any, do you need to make to honor these values?

____

____

____

____

Task: Vision Commitment

Write a vision statement. Place it where you'll see it daily.

MY VISION STATEMENT

Module 9
Right People: Community & Success

Relationship Audit

List the people in your life and categorize them as "positive influence" or "toxic influence."

Positive Influence

Toxic Influence

Reflection Questions

How can you strengthen positive connections and set boundaries with toxic ones?

Task: Build a Support Network

Reach out to a mentor or join a supportive community this week.

Module 10
Gratitude and Giving: Fueling Success

Exercise 1: Gratitude List
Write down three things you're grateful for each day for one week.

I am GRATEFUL for...

1. _______________________________
2. _______________________________
3. _______________________________

Reflection Question
How has focusing on gratitude impacted your mindset?

____

____

____

____

____

____

Task: Giving Back

Identify a cause you care about. Volunteer or donate to it this month.

Module 11
Fear to Freedom: Embrace Imperfection

Exercise 1: Imperfect Action Plan

Choose one task you've been procrastinating on. Commit to completing it this week, even if imperfect.

Reflection Question

How did letting go of perfection feel?

Task: Reflect on Failure

Write about a failure. Identify what you learned and how it shaped you.

Module 12

Finding Courage: Empowering Others

Exercise 1: Mentorship Map

Identify one person you can mentor or support.

- *Write their name and one specific action you can take to help them build courage.*

....

....

....

....

Reflection Question

What lessons from your journey can inspire others?

....

....

....

....

Task: Share Your Story

Write or verbally share one experience where you found courage.

- Reflect on the impact your story could have on others.

____

____

____

____

____

____

____

Reflection Question

How does mentoring or sharing your story make you feel?

____

____

____

____

____

____

Module 13

Bet on Yourself:
Rewards & Growth

Exercise 1: Confidence Journal

Write about a time you took a risk and succeeded.

Answer:

- What gave you the courage to take the risk?

- What did you learn from this experience?

....

....

....

....

....

Task: Take a Small Risk

Choose a situation where you can step slightly out of your comfort zone this week.

- Reflect on the outcome and how it impacted your confidence.

....

....

....

Reflection Question

What is one way you can continue betting on yourself daily?

Resilience Through Change: Embrace & Adapt

Exercise 1: Resilience Reflection

Reflect on a recent setback.

- Write three ways it challenged you and three ways it helped you grow.

Three Ways It CHALLENGED You

____

____

____

____

Three Ways It HELPED You GROW

____

____

____

____

____

Task: Build a Resilience Toolkit

Create a list of strategies to build resilience during tough times:

Mindfulness Techniques

Physical Activity

Journaling Prompts

Support Network

Affirmations

Reflection Question

How can you use these tools to navigate future challenges?

Exercise 1: Impact Goals

Identify one way you'd like to make a lasting impact in your family, community, or field.

- Outline the first steps to achieve this goal.

Task: Legacy Action Plan

Choose one legacy-building action to complete this month, such as:

- Mentoring someone
- Starting a project or tradition
- Donating time or resources to a cause

Reflection Question

What does leaving a legacy mean to you personally?

Module 16
Purpose-Filled Life: Reflections & Growth

Exercise 1: Purpose-Filled Goals

Identify three important lessons you learned throughout your journey. How did these lessons impact your life, and what did you take away from those experiences?

....

....

....

....

Task: Gratitude and Intention

Here are three specific actions you can take to help others. Record your observations as you try one or all of the following activities.

- Host a Free Monthly Live Story Session —During these sessions, share a personal life lesson, such as overcoming fear or rebuilding after loss. Share the lessons via a Zoom or Instagram Live. End each session with an actionable takeaway and open Q&A to support others in similar situations.

....

....

....

....

- Write "Letters of Light" Series — Draft short, heartfelt letters or blog posts addressed to people facing struggles you've overcome (e.g., "To the woman Starting Over After Divorce"). Publish them on your website, social media, or Medium.

- Create a "Pay-It-Forward Resource Kit" — Bundle a free digital download (e.g., journaling prompts, a healing playlist, or a checklist for a fresh start) and encourage recipients to share it with one friend or a community in need. Include your story as a preface.

Reflection Question

What lasting feelings remain after embarking on this journey?

Conclusion
Embracing the Journey

Final Exercise: The Life Purpose Statement

Using insights from this workbook, write a one-paragraph statement summarizing your purpose, vision, and commitment to growth.

Reflection Question

How will you continue to build confidence and level up beyond this workbook?

CONFIDENCE
IN ACTION

A Step-by-Step Guide to Leveling UP